THE WALRUS AND THE CARPENTER

Lewis Carroll

THE WALRUS AND THE CARPENTER

Illustrations by Jane Breskin Zalben

With Annotations by Tweedledee and Tweedledum

BOYDS MILLS PRESS

As always, for Alexander and Jonathan—
Two pearls in my oyster,
With all my love

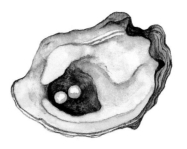

Published by Caroline House
Boyds Mills Press, Inc.
A Highlights Company
815 Church Street
Honesdale, Pennsylvania 18431
Printed in China

Publisher Cataloging-in-Publication Data
Carroll, Lewis, 1832-1898
The walrus and the carpenter : poems for children / by Lewis Carroll ;
illustrated by Jane Breskin Zalben.
[32]p. : col. ill. ; cm.
Originally published by Henry Holt and Co.: N.Y., 1986.
Summary: A walrus and a carpenter encounter some oysters during their walk
on the beach—an unfortunate meeting for the oysters.
ISBN 1-56397-719-2 (pb)
1. Nonsense verses, English. 2. Children's poetry, English. [1. Nonsense verses.
2. English poetry.] I. Zalben, Jane Breskin, ill. II. Walrus and the carpenter. III. Title.
821.52—dc21   1986   AC   CIP
Library of Congress Catalog Card Number 85-7591

First Boyds Mills Press paperback edition, 1998
The illustrations were done in watercolor and colored pencil.
The text was set in Egmont Medium.
10 9 8 7 6 5 4 3 2 1

FOREWORD

What if it had been called "The Walrus and the Butterfly"? Or "The Walrus and the Baronet"? While writing *Through the Looking-Glass and What Alice Found There* (1871), a sequel to *Alice's Adventures in Wonderland* (1865), Lewis Carroll had decided on the Walrus for the poem, but gave his illustrator John Tenniel the choice of drawing a "butterfly," "baronet," or "carpenter." It did not matter to him. Each fit the meter perfectly!

Evidently, as far as writing nonsense poetry was concerned, Carroll believed in twisting around the Ugly Duchess' nutty advice to Alice, "Take care of the sounds, and the sense will take care of itself!" Incongruity lies at the heart of humor. Tenniel, however, came to regret his rather rash decision in choosing a carpenter over a butterfly or baronet. While working on the pictures, he informed Carroll that he found "the Walrus and the Carpenter a hopeless combination" and begged to have the Carpenter abolished! It was a bit late; but, "to suit the artist," Carroll did alter the second line of the poem from "Were walking *hand-in-hand*" to "Were walking *close at hand*." It did not matter to him.

Unfortunately, the Ugly Duchesses of the world insist, "Tut, tut, child! Everything's got a moral, if only you can find it." They cannot accept nonsense for what it is—*nonsense*. They argue that "The Walrus and the Carpenter" must mean *something!* Many people believe that the verse was in some way a parody of Thomas Hood's "The Dream of Eugene Aram, the Murderer;" but Carroll said otherwise. "In writing 'The Walrus and the Carpenter,'" he explained, "I had no particular poem in mind. The meter is a common one, and I don't think 'Eugene Aram' suggested it more than the many other poems I have read in in the same meter." Again the sounds were taking care of the sense. Not everyone believed him. Some are still convinced that it must have been a political allegory. Carroll's friend, Henry Kingsley, suggested in the novel *Valentin* (1872) that the poem was a satire of the Franco-Prussian War. J. B. Priestly in *the New*

Statesman (Aug. 10, 1957) considered the Walrus and the Carpenter archetypes of certain kinds of politicians. But nonsense does not mean—it is!

"The Walrus and the Carpenter" is one of the masterpieces of nonsense poetry and one of the best poems Lewis Carroll ever wrote. "Jabberwocky" is its only equal. Some lines of "The Walrus and the Carpenter" are known by everybody. William Sydney Porter (O. Henry)́, for one, took its most famous phrase for the title of his first collection of short stories, *Cabbages and Kings* (1904).

It is a wonder that more picture books have not been made of this classic verse. Jane Breskin Zalben, who did similar service to Carroll's *Jabberwocky* (1977), is one of the few artists who has dared challenge Sir John Tenniel's famous wood-engraved interpretations with her modern watercolors. The American illustrator has taken the Walrus and the Carpenter of Tenniel's solid, stolid, matter-of-fact manner and returned them to a child's midsummer reverie. She has removed the nightmare from behind the Looking-Glass. Sea, sky, and shore all wash together in the translucent, limpid colors of some undefined dreamscape. Zalben has turned Carroll's nonsense poem into a lullaby.

Yet she provides some pathos missing from other interpretations of the poem. Who, except one who laughs at the death of Dickens' Little Nell, cannot but feel some sorrow for the Oysters' sad fate from the pitiful little Mary Janes, jogging shoes, and jellies left on the beach? Other children will be just as puzzled as Alice whether to like the Walrus (who hid the number he ate) or the Carpenter (who ate as many as he could) better. Whom do *you* favor?

Michael Patrick Hearn

With Annotations by Tweedledee and Tweedledum

"You like poetry?"

"Ye-es, pretty well—*some* poetry," Alice said doubtfully. "Would you tell me which road leads out of the wood?"

"What shall I repeat to her?" said Tweedledee, looking round at Tweedledum with great solemn eyes, and not noticing Alice's question.

" *'The Walrus and the Carpenter'* is the longest," Tweedledum replied, giving his brother an affectionate hug.

Tweedledee began instantly:

"The sun was shining—"

Here Alice ventured to interrupt him. "If it's *very* long," she said, as politely as she could, "would you please tell me first which road—"

Tweedledee smiled gently, and began again:

The sun was shining on the sea,
   Shining with all his might:
He did his very best to make
   The billows smooth and bright—
And this was odd, because it was
   The middle of the night.

The moon was shining sulkily,
    Because she thought the sun
Had got no business to be there
    After the day was done—
'It's very rude of him,' she said,
    'To come and spoil the fun!'

The sea was wet as wet could be,
　The sands were dry as dry.
You could not see a cloud, because
　No cloud was in the sky:
No birds were flying overhead—
　There were no birds to fly.

The Walrus and the Carpenter
Were walking close at hand:
They wept like anything to see
Such quantities of sand:
'If this were only cleared away,'
They said, 'it would be grand!'

'If seven maids with seven mops
    Swept it for half a year,
Do you suppose,' the Walrus said,
    'That they could get it clear?'
'I doubt it,' said the Carpenter,
    And shed a bitter tear.

'O Oysters, come and walk with us!'
  The Walrus did beseech.
'A pleasant walk, a pleasant talk,
  Along the briny beach:
We cannot do with more than four,
  To give a hand to each.'

The eldest Oyster looked at him,
But never a word he said:
The eldest Oyster winked his eye,
And shook his heavy head—
Meaning to say he did not choose
To leave the oyster-bed.

But four young Oysters hurried up,
    All eager for the treat:
Their coats were brushed, their faces washed,
    Their shoes were clean and neat—
And this was odd, because, you know,
    They hadn't any feet.
Four other Oysters followed them,
    And yet another four;
And thick and fast they came at last,
    And more, and more, and more—
All hopping through the frothy waves,
    And scrambling to the shore.

The Walrus and the Carpenter
Walked on a mile or so,
And then they rested on a rock
Conveniently low:
And all the little Oysters stood
And waited in a row.

'The time has come,' the Walrus said,
    'To talk of many things:
Of shoes—and ships—and sealing-wax—

Of cabbages—and kings—
And why the sea is boiling hot—
And whether pigs have wings.'

'But wait a bit,' the Oysters cried,
   'Before we have our chat;
For some of us are out of breath,
   And all of us are fat!'
'No hurry!' said the Carpenter.
   They thanked him much for that.

'A loaf of bread,' the Walrus said,
　'Is what we chiefly need:
Pepper and vinegar besides
　Are very good indeed—
Now, if you're ready, Oysters dear,
　We can begin to feed.'

'But not on us!' the Oysters cried,
    Turning a little blue.
'After such kindness, that would be
    A dismal thing to do!'
'The night is fine,' the Walrus said.
    'Do you admire the view?

'It was so kind of you to come!
    And you are very nice!'
The Carpenter said nothing but
    'Cut us another slice.
I wish you were not quite so deaf—
    I've had to ask you twice!'
'It seems a shame,' the Walrus said,
    'To play them such a trick.
After we've brought them out so far,
    And made them trot so quick!'
The Carpenter said nothing but
    'The butter's spread too thick!'

'I weep for you.' the Walrus said:
      'I deeply sympathize.'
With sobs and tears he sorted out
      Those of the largest size,
Holding his pocket-handkerchief
      Before his streaming eyes.

'O Oysters,' said the Carpenter,
  'You've had a pleasant run!
Shall we be trotting home again?'
  But answer came there none—
And this was scarcely odd, because
  They'd eaten every one.''

Through the Looking-Glass

"I like the Walrus best," said Alice: "because he was a *little* sorry for the poor oysters."

"He ate more than the Carpenter, though," said Tweedledee. "You see he held his handkerchief in front, so that the Carpenter couldn't count how many he took: contrariwise."

"That was mean!" Alice said indignantly. "Then I like the Carpenter best—if he didn't eat so many as the Walrus."

"But he ate as many as he could get," said Tweedledum.

This was a puzzler. After a pause, Alice began, "Well! They were *both* very unpleasant characters—"